# OH! THOSE CRAZY DOGS!

## TEDDI BEAR COMES HOME

**BOOK TWO**

**CAL**

Illustrated by Rachael Plaquet

To order additional copies of this book, contact:
Xlibris
844-714-8691
www.Xlibris.com
Orders@Xlibris.com

ISBN: 978-1-6641-9065-8 (sc)
ISBN: 978-1-6641-9066-5 (hc)
ISBN: 978-1-6641-9064-1 (e)

Library of Congress Control Number:
2021917156

Print information available on the last page

Rev. date: 08/27/2021

# Introduction

This is a story about 2 crazy dogs, their adventures and the mischief they get into.

They are very loving dogs, but they can't help getting into things.

Hi ! I'm Colby! I'm big and red and furry ! I love everyone but sometimes people are afraid of me because I am so big!

Hi ! I'm Teddy Bear! I'm big and white and very furry! I'm not as big as Colby, but just about. Everyone thinks I'm cute and I put shows on for them.

Our owners picked us out specially and brought us home to love and care for us. We love them too, very much. They give us everything and a warm loving home. We will call them Mom and Pop

Sometimes we don't listen to them, especially me, Teddi Bear!

but our Mom and Pop love us anyway. Sometimes I get Colby in trouble. I can get him to do anything I want because he loves me too and can't say no. He protects me all the time.

# TEDDI BEAR COMING HOME !

On a cold snowy, stormy day, I was chasing my brother around the pen that we shared in the kennel we lived in.

A lady came in and asked my caretaker to see one of the pups that had been on a computer. The lady came into the pen area and watched us chase each other around and around really fast.

The two pups looked exactly the same.

The lady asked the caretaker if she could pick them up because they were going so fast she couldn't tell which one was which. The caretaker picked us up with some difficulty because we were squirmy.

We wanted to run and play! The lady said, "That's the one I want." she said and she picked me!

My brother was sad because he was all alone now.

My mom brought me to her van, and there was a great big red dog in it. He started barking.

But then mom said, "Shh Colby, I have brought you a baby brother."

She said, "Look how sweet he is." Colby stopped barking and started sniffing me and he poked  me with his nose!

poke, poke, sniff, sniff.

He gave me a couple of licks, and he seemed to like me.

My caretaker told the lady I wouldn't grow as big as Colby but just about. I was about as big as Colby's head right now.

My mom put me in a box on the seat beside her and said goodbye to the caretaker. It was still snowing a bit, but we went slow. I kept standing up and looking out of the box to see where we were going.

Then I would lie down again and stand up again to look out the window.

My new mom kept laughing at me and called me a jack-in-the-box. I would wag my tail when she would laugh.

One time I jumped up and looked out the window, and there was another car beside us. The people inside were pointing at me and laughing.

I kept jumping up and down and wagged my tail. My new mom said, "You are making everyone smile and laugh today." We finally got to my new home, and Mom took me out of the van, and Colby followed.

We went through a garage and up some stairs into a hall. I sniffed a room that smelled very good.

But we didn't go in there. Mom said, "We are going upstairs to the family room where you will spend most of your time with Colby."

There was a doggy bed in there, so I ran and jumped right into it.

Colby looked at me in the bed and gave a little growl.

I guessed he was trying to tell me that was his bed, but I stayed there anyway.

Colby jumped on the big couch, so he was very comfortable too.

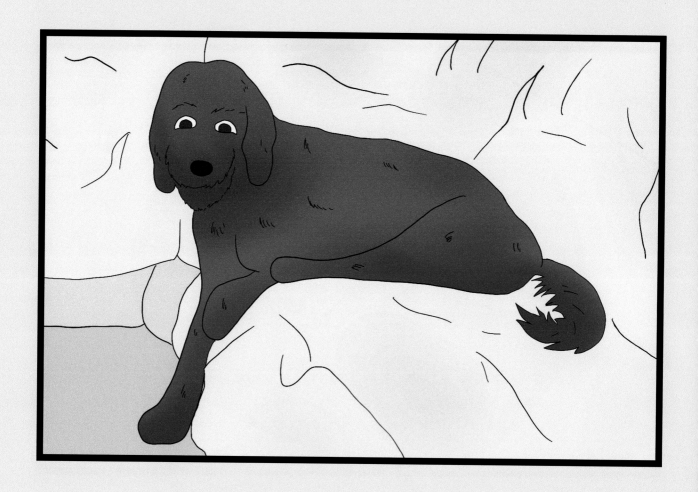

I had a nice nap, and then Pop picked me up and brought me outside into a fenced in area and said, "This is where you go pee." He put me down, and I peed right away because I had to go pee. Pop said, "Good boy, good boy," and I wagged my tail.

He brought me back in the house and up into the family room where Colby was.

I saw that Colby would go to the door leading to the pen and just bark, and they would bring him to the pen to do his business.

Anytime we would go into the backyard, they would open a gate so we could go into the pen to pee if we needed to. We were not allowed to pee in the yard.

One day, Colby had a great big bone. He was lying on the large chair and chewing it.

That bone was bigger than me.

I tried to reach up to the top of the couch to get the bone, but I couldn't reach. I jumped and jumped but couldn't reach it.

I think Colby was laughing at me, and Mom and Pop too.

I just sat there for a while and watched him chew it. Then I went to find some toys to play with. They were all Colby's toys, but that was okay. He didn't seem to mind that I played with them.

Soon he came over and started to play with me too. We played tug-of-war with the big tug toy.

I thought he let me win because he was so much bigger and stronger than me. We would wrestle, and Colby would roll over on his back and let me jump all over him.

He would let me bite at him all over, but I didn't ever hurt him, and Colby was always so gentle. He would hold me with his front paws and roll over with me on him.

We had so much fun! Colby let me do anything I wanted. My mom and pop would play with us a lot and laugh.

My tail was always wagging. I was so happy and having so much fun.

My mom would always hug me, but I would squirm away and continue playing.

I was a crazy, playing dog! Colby and I just ran around and around the big room.

And when Colby had enough, he would just jump on one of the couches.

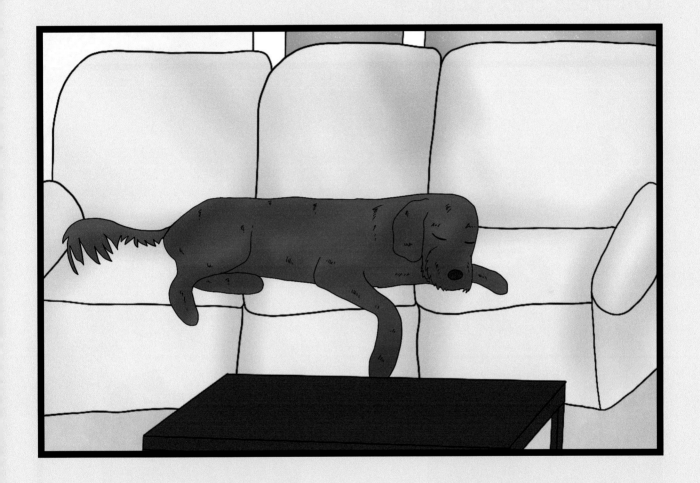

And I couldn't reach him. Mom and Pop just laughed and said,

"Oh those crazy puppies!"

Look for book 3 where Teddi Bear and
Colby have more adventures!

Books Written By **CAL**

## Oh! Those Crazy Dogs! Series

Book 1  Colby Comes Home

Book 2  Teddi Bear Comes Home

Book 3  Coming soon! Watch for it!